Prem: Ek Sookha Phool

Aayush Maatrishya

Maatrishya

Contents

Foreword

In the pages that follow, you will discover a love story that is both timeless and contemporary, a tale of two souls entwined in the intricate dance of tradition, love, and sacrifice. *"Prem: Ek Sookha Phool"* is not just a story but a profound exploration of love's enduring power.

Ananya and Sameer's story is a testament to the richness of human emotion, where love knows no boundaries, transcending the constraints of time, place, and culture. It is a narrative that resonates with anyone who has faced the exquisite joy and searing pain of love, making their journey universally relatable.

As the pages turn, you will be transported into the lives of Ananya and Sameer, two individuals who dared to defy convention for the sake of love. Their love story unfolds against the backdrop of a changing world, where tradition and modernity often collide, leaving us to question the choices we make in the name of love and duty.

Through their journey, we are reminded that love is not always straightforward, that it often demands great sacrifices, and that it can inspire us to challenge the very fabric of our lives. Ananya and Sameer's story encapsulates the essence of love—the profound connection between two souls that can withstand even the harshest of storms.

This is a story of love's enduring strength and its ability to bridge the deepest divides. It is a story of resilience, as Ananya and Sameer face trials that test the limits of their devotion. It is a story of hope, showing us that love can thrive even in the most challenging of circumstances.

As you delve into these pages, may you find inspiration in the love that knows no boundaries, and may you be reminded that, in matters of the heart, the most profound truths often lie in the spaces between tradition and individuality, family and self, and love and sacrifice.

We invite you to immerse yourself in the world of Ananya and Sameer, to witness their journey of love, and to reflect on the boundaries, both real and imagined, that love can traverse. Their story is a beacon, guiding us through the complexities of life and love, showing us that, in the end, it is love that truly matters.

Introduction

In a world where tradition often collides with the boundless depths of the heart, the story of Ananya and Sameer unfolds a testament to the power of love that defies all odds. Their journey takes us through the intricate tapestry of their lives, where love, culture, and personal dreams clash and converge in a compelling narrative that resonates with the human spirit.

Ananya, a spirited young woman, carries the weight of her family's expectations and the richness of her cultural heritage. Her heart, however, knows no boundaries when it comes to love. Sameer, a kindred spirit, enters her life like a shooting star, igniting a passion that transcends the confines of tradition and social norms.

As they navigate the complexities of their love story, we follow their footsteps through the bustling streets of the city, the serene moments in their cherished park, and the tearful goodbyes that threaten to sever their connection. Their love, pure and profound, faces the ultimate test as they grapple with the stark choice between honoring their families' traditions and following their hearts' desires.

Their tale is a vivid portrayal of the profound emotions, the heart-wrenching decisions, and the unwavering commitment that bind them together. Join us as we delve deeper into the chapters of their extraordinary love story, where love conquers boundaries and souls are forever intertwined.

Preface

In the tapestry of human existence, there are tales that stand out as remarkable testaments to the resilience of the human heart. *"Prem: Ek Sookha Phool"* is one such story. It weaves together the threads of tradition and passion, love and sacrifice, family and individuality, in a narrative that transcends geographical and cultural boundaries.

Ananya, a young woman of deep cultural roots, finds herself torn between her love for Sameer and the expectations of her traditional family. The clash between her heart's desires and her family's values sets the stage for a poignant and heartfelt exploration of the choices we make in the name of love.

Sameer, a symbol of unwavering devotion and understanding, embarks on a journey alongside Ananya, one that will test the very core of their love. Their tale unfolds against the backdrop of a bustling city, a serene park where their love bloomed, and the inevitable goodbyes that threaten to pull them apart.

As we journey through the pages of their story, we are reminded that love is not confined by boundaries, customs, or societal norms. It is a force that can bridge the widest gaps and transcend the deepest divisions. Ananya and Sameer's love story serves as an enduring testament to the power of love to conquer all, to unite souls in the face of adversity, and to inspire us to follow our hearts.

In the following chapters, we will delve into the intricacies of their relationship, the challenges they face, and the choices they must make. Their journey is a reflection of the human experience, where love, in all its forms, remains the most potent and transformative force.

Join us as we embark on this emotional and heartfelt journey, guided by the love story of Ananya and Sameer, where boundaries are shattered, and hearts are forever intertwined.

Prologue

In a world where love often finds itself entangled in the intricate web of tradition, culture, and family expectations, the story of Ananya and Sameer emerges as a powerful testament to the indomitable force of the human heart.

This is a tale of two souls drawn together by an irresistible connection, a love story that defies the boundaries imposed by society. Ananya, a young woman of grace and determination, finds herself caught between her family's deep-rooted traditions and her heart's longing for a love that transcends convention. Sameer, a man of unwavering devotion and profound love, becomes the beacon of hope in her tumultuous journey.

As we journey through the chapters of their lives, we will witness the trials they face, the sacrifices they make, and the strength of their love, which refuses to waver in the face of adversity. Their love story takes us on a rollercoaster ride of emotions, from the heights of passion to the depths of despair, as they navigate the challenging waters of love, family, and self-discovery.

"Prem: Ek Sookha Phool" is a story that will tug at your heartstrings, making you question the boundaries that society often places on matters of the heart. It is a narrative that explores the complexities of love, the clash between tradition and individuality, and the enduring power of the human spirit.

In the pages that follow, you will be transported into a world where love knows no boundaries, where two souls dare to defy convention for the sake of love, and where the bonds of family and tradition are tested against the unstoppable force of the heart's desires.

Join us on this extraordinary journey, where love unfolds amidst the backdrop of a changing world, and where the choices made in the name of love have the power to transform lives forever.

A Call of Destiny

In the heart of Soumya Lok, a poignant story unfolded that would forever leave an indelible mark on a young boy named Sameer, who was in his late twenties.

It was a quiet evening, the sun setting in hues of orange and gold, casting a warm glow over Sameer's modest home. He sat engrossed in his studies when the phone rang, shattering the tranquility of the moment.

His mother, a woman with worry etched into her voice, hurriedly answered. *"Beta, Nanaji se baat karlo, Jaldi se,"* she implored. *"Bahut serious condition hai wo hospital me hain"*.

The phone call hung heavy in the air as his mother cut the line. A sense of foreboding washed over Sameer, and he began to shiver. His nanaji, his beloved grandfather, was the closest person in his life.

The tears welled up in his eyes as he tried to call his grandfather. The call was answered by a gentle voice, that of a doctor. He inquired about Sameer's name, and when Sameer mentioned he was his maternal grandchild, the doctor's tone softened. *"Woh subah se hi tumse baat karna chahte hain, Tumhra naam liye ja rahe the,"* the doctor explained.

With a mixture of anxiety and anticipation, Sameer waited for his nanaji to come on the line. *"Arre Sameer, kaise ho,"* his nanaji's voice, although filled with warmth, held a hint of weakness.

Sameer struggled to hold back his tears. *"Tabiyat thodi si kharab ho gayi hai,"* his nanaji confided.

Choking back his emotions, Sameer reassured him, *"Are nahi-nahi kuchh nahi hua hai aap chinta mt kijiye."*

His nanaji's voice, although feeble, was laced with wisdom. *"Ha abhi hum hai, jab tak tumko doctor bante nahi dekh lete Marenge thodi hum, tum inlog ka baat mat suno,"* he said, tears streaming down from his face. *"Padhai karo achhe se, aur jaldi se doctor bano."*

His nanaji's voice trembled, but it was filled with unwavering faith and love. *"Aur ek baat yaad rakhna agar hm kal nahi bhi rehte hain to, Humko tumpe bahut Garv aur bharosa hai, Koi kare ya nahi, hum tumpe hamesha Garv krenge,"* he said his words heavy with emotion. *"Jao padhai kro ab."*

Sameer, with his tall frame and warm, expressive eyes, carried himself with a quiet confidence that spoke volumes about his resilience.

Growing up in a close-knit community, Sameer was known not only for his academic dedication but also for his unwavering commitment to his family.

His mother, a strong and resilient woman, had raised him single-handedly, teaching him the values of compassion and perseverance.

As a child, Sameer often spent his afternoons listening to his nanaji's stories about his days as a dedicated physician. Dr. Rajan Kapoor's tales of healing, empathy and the impact of medical care on people's lives left an indelible impression on young Sameer's mind.

These stories ignited a spark within him, planting the seeds of a dream that would shape his future.. But dreams, especially those of becoming a doctor, came with their own set of challenges. Sameer's family faced financial constraints that threatened to extinguish the flickering flame of his aspirations.

Undeterred, he took on part-time jobs, tutoring other students, and working long hours to support his education. These trials only strengthened his resolve to overcome adversity and reach his goals.

In addition to his academic pursuits, Sameer actively participated in medical missions to remote villages, providing healthcare to underserved communities.

These experiences exposed him to the stark realities of healthcare disparities, motivating him to not only achieve his dreams but also to make a meaningful impact on the lives of those who lacked access to medical care.
Sameer's journey was not just about becoming a doctor; it was about fulfilling a promise to his beloved nanaji, carrying forward his legacy of compassion and service.

As we follow Sameer's path, we will witness the challenges and triumphs that shape his destiny and lead him toward a future where the healing touch of a dedicated doctor can make all the difference.

Shadows of Self-Doubt

Ananya, the central character in our tale, embodies the essence of a poet's soul—a vibrant symphony in human form. However, her journey as a poet is not without its trials and tribulations.

The persistent shadow of creative self-doubt often looms over Ananya, causing her to question the worthiness of her poetic expressions. There are moments when she feels her verses fall short of capturing the depth of her emotions, leading to frustration and despondency.

The path of a poet can be a solitary one, and Ananya frequently grapples with isolation. Her dedication to her craft compels her to retreat into the recesses of her thoughts and the pages of her notebook, seeking solace while simultaneously battling loneliness.

Financial constraints add another layer of complexity to her artistic journey. Poetry, though rich in artistic value, often offers limited financial returns. Ananya must strike a delicate balance between her artistic pursuits and the demands of everyday life, occasionally taking on odd jobs to make ends meet.

Nevertheless, Ananya perseveres. Her profound love for poetry, unwavering belief in the transformative power of her words, and unrelenting dedication to her craft serve as the driving forces behind her determination. She continues to pour her heart and soul into her verses, sharing her poetry with the world even when the path ahead seems steep and challenging.

Ananya's struggles as a poet are not mere obstacles; they are integral components of her artistic journey. These challenges mold her resilience and deepen her connection to her craft, each one serving as a stepping stone, a wellspring of inspiration, and a testament to her unwavering commitment to the art of poetry.

Amidst the trials and tribulations of her poetic journey, Ananya discovers solace in late-night conversations with her confidante, Tanya. These talks become a lifeline, offering encouragement and understanding in the face of creative adversity.

Tanya, brimming with enthusiasm and possessing an acute ear for poetry, is Ananya's steadfast companion. Their rendezvous at a favorite café, where the aroma of freshly brewed coffee mingles with the scent of well-worn books, provides the backdrop for their intimate conversations.

During these late-night talks, Ananya bares her insecurities about her poetry, confessing how self-doubt can stifle her creativity. Tanya, a true friend and a poet in her own right, responds with unwavering belief, akin to a gentle breeze calming a storm.

"Ananya, teri kavitaon mein dil ko hila dene aur parivartan laane mein saksham hai." Tanya affirms, her eyes brimming with conviction. *"Har mahan kavi samay-samay par sandeh ke palon ka samna karte hain; yahi pal hain jab aap apni asli awaz ko dhoondhte hain."*

Ananya often recites her latest verses aloud to Tanya, who listens intently. These talks evolve into discussions exploring the themes, metaphors, and emotions woven into Ananya's poetry. Tanya's insightful feedback becomes a guiding light, enabling Ananya to refine her craft and unearth new depths within her work.

Tanya reminds her, *"Tumhara struggles ek kavi ke safar ka ek important part hain—ye tumhari kalpana ki tasveer mein buni hui dor hain. Inhe apnalo, kyunki inhi se ant mein tu ujwal ho payegi."*

Through these late-night talks, Ananya not only discovers a trusted friend but also a muse, mentor, and an unending source of inspiration. Their conversations serve as a testament to the enduring power of friendship and the profound influence it wields upon one's creative odyssey.

Silent Talks in the Village

In a small, remote village nestled amidst lush green fields and rolling hills, two kindred spirits, Sameer and Ananya, were destined to cross paths. This quaint village, untouched by the hustle and bustle of modern life, held the secrets of a slower, more contemplative existence.

Sameer had arrived in the village as part of a volunteer medical mission. He was a dedicated medical student, passionate about serving communities that lacked access to healthcare. With a backpack filled with medical supplies and a heart brimming with compassion, he set out on a journey to make a difference.

Ananya, on the other hand, was seeking inspiration for her poetry. The village, with its pristine landscapes and untouched beauty, called out to her artistic soul. She hoped to find a connection between nature and her verses, breathing life into her poetry with the simplicity and authenticity of rural life.

Their paths first crossed on a serene morning by the village well. Sameer was busy attending to the healthcare needs of the villagers, his kind demeanor and warm smile earning him their trust. He moved with a quiet grace, listening intently to their ailments and offering reassurance.

Ananya, with her notebook in hand, observed this scene from a distance. She was captivated not only by the doctor's dedication but also by the interactions between him and the villagers. The depth of his empathy left an indelible mark on her.

Days turned into weeks, and Sameer continued his work in the village, forging deep connections with the locals. He learned about their way of life, their struggles, and their dreams. Ananya, too, began to immerse herself in the village's rhythms, finding inspiration in its simplicity.

One evening, as the sun painted the sky with hues of orange and pink, Ananya sat by the village well, her notebook open before her. She tried to capture the essence of the village in her verses but found herself at a creative impasse. The words refused to flow.

Sameer, who had just finished tending to a patient, noticed Ananya's contemplative expression. He approached her, his footsteps as soft as the whispers of the wind through the fields. He didn't say a word, for he understood the sacredness of silence.

Ananya looked up, meeting Sameer's kind eyes. In that shared moment of silence, they connected on a profound level. It was as though their souls spoke a language beyond words, a language of empathy, understanding, and shared purpose.

As the days passed, their paths continued to intersect. They often found themselves sitting by the village well, side by side, in companionable silence. Ananya's poetry began to flow effortlessly, infused with the beauty of the village and the empathy she saw in Sameer's actions.

Sameer, too, discovered a newfound source of inspiration in Ananya's verses. Her words painted vivid images of the village, its people, and the serenity of rural life. He admired her passion for her craft and the way she captured the world's essence in her poetry.

Their connection deepened with each passing day, transcending the need for spoken words. They had found in each other a kindred spirit, a source of inspiration, and a silent companion on their respective journeys.

When the time came for Sameer to bid farewell to the village, Ananya's heart ached. Yet, she knew that their connection, forged in the serenity of the village and nurtured in the language of silence, would forever remain a cherished chapter in their lives.

As Sameer departed, he left behind a part of his heart in the village, carrying with him the memory of a poet whose verses spoke to his soul. And Ananya continued to create poetry that echoed the essence of the village, forever touched by the doctor who had shown her the beauty of empathy without words.

Their meeting, in a village where silence spoke volumes, became a testament to the profound connections that can be formed when hearts resonate in harmony, even without uttering a single word.

Fateful Meeting among the Shelves

After their inspiring and transformative experience organizing a health camp in the remote village, Sameer and Ananya returned to the bustling city, each carrying a sense of fulfillment and a stronger connection to their shared passion for making a positive impact on the world.

One sunny afternoon, Sameer decided to visit the local library to unwind and reflect on the recent village campaign. The library, with its rows of bookshelves and the soft rustling of pages turning, had always been a sanctuary for him. As he entered, he couldn't help but smile, thinking about the children he had met in the village and how he had shared his love for reading with them.

Unbeknownst to Sameer, Ananya had also decided to visit the library that day. Her heart was still brimming with the joy of using her artistic talents to engage the village children and spread awareness about health and hygiene. She wanted to find books that could help her further inspire the children she had met.

As Sameer perused the shelves filled with books of all genres, he noticed a section on community service and healthcare. Intrigued, he began exploring the titles, hoping to find resources that might be useful for their future campaigns.

Just a few bookshelves away, Ananya was engrossed in the art section, looking for books that would help her refine her artistic skills and create more impactful visual aids for their campaigns. As she reached for a book on art techniques, her hand brushed against Sameer's, who was reaching for a book on public health.

Their eyes met, and recognition flashed across their faces. It was the same feeling they had experienced in the village, the unspoken connection of kindred spirits brought together by their shared passion for making a difference in the world.

Ananya's eyes lit up with a familiar enthusiasm. *"Arey aap, pehchana?"* she exclaimed.

Sameer, equally delighted, replied, *"Haan, kaise nahi pehchaunga, aap campaign mein thi, aur itni achi kavita jo likhti hai,"* Ananya enquired, *"Aapko kaise pata ki mein achhi kavita likhti hun?"* Sameer said, *"Arey han, aap achhi kavita kaise likh sakti hain,"* (Laughing), *"mazak kar raha hoon, gaon ke bacchon ne aapki kavita 'Asadh mein savan' sunai aur sach baataon to mujhe bahut pasand aayi".* *"Iske liye aapka shukriya,"* Ananya said.

Ananya, her eyes filled with curiosity, asked Sameer, *"Aaj aap library aaye hain? Lagta hai Kuch dilchasp kitaaben dhoondh rahe hain aap?"* Sameer, still in awe of how their paths had crossed once more, replied, *"Oh! mein asal mein community healthcare se related kitaben dhundh raha tha. Gaon mein hamare campaign ke baad, mein hamare agle campaign ke liye behtar taiyar hona chahta hoon."*

They began to chat, sharing stories of their experiences in the village and their dedication to community service. Sameer was impressed by Ananya's artistic talents and her ability to connect with the children through her creativity. Ananya admired Sameer's commitment to healthcare and his determination to make a positive impact.

Hours passed by in the bookstore, but for Sameer and Ananya, it felt like mere minutes. They decided to continue their conversation over a cup of coffee at a nearby café.

As they continued their conversation, Sameer suggested they collaborate on future campaigns, combining their skills to create more engaging and effective initiatives. Ananya agreed wholeheartedly, excited about the prospect of working together.

Their chance meeting in the library had not only rekindled the spark they had felt in the village but had also set the stage for a powerful partnership. Sameer and Ananya, brought together once again by fate and their shared passion for making a difference, were ready to embark on a new chapter of their journey, using their unique talents to create positive change in the world.

Ananya's Cafe Confessions

Ananya sat across from her close friend Tanya at their favorite café, a steaming cup of chai in hand, ready to share the latest developments in her life. Tanya, with a mischievous twinkle in her eyes, couldn't help but sense that something was different this time.

"Thik hai, batao sab kuch, Ananya," Tanya said, leaning forward. *"Mein samajh sakti hoon ki tumhare mann mein kuch baat hai, aur yeh sirf woh nayi poem collection nahi hai jis par tum kaam kar rahi ho."*

Ananya blushed slightly, her cheeks taking on a rosy hue. *"Well, Tanya, tum yakinan nahi karogi, lekin maine hal hi mein ek, incredible person se mili. Uska naam Sameer hai, aur woh sirf healthcare and community services mein interest nahi rakhta hain, balki woh bahut kind and thoughtful bhi hai".*

Tanya couldn't resist a teasing smile. *"Oh, sach mein? Sameer? Kya yeh wahi Sameer hai jo gaon ke campaign mein tha?"*

Ananya nodded, trying to downplay her excitement. *"Haan, wohi Sameer hai. Lekin Tanya, yeh woh nahi hai jo tum soch rahi ho. Hum sirf dost hain, ham sirf volunteer work mein partners hain. Hamare beech mein kuch romantic nahi hai."*

Tanya chuckled softly. *"Ananya, main tumhe saalon se jaanti hoon, aur mujhe samajh mein aata hai yahan dosti se zyada kuch ho raha hai. Kya tum sure ho ki tumhara dil kuch nahi keh raha ya phir ye tumhara mann ka khel to nahi hai?"*

Ananya sighed, realizing she might not convince her friend easily. *"Tanya, mein tumhe sach keh rahi hoon, Sameer aur main sirf dost hain. We share a deep connection through our shared passions and goals. lekin isse zyada kuch nahi hai."*

"So, Ananya," Tanya began with a sly grin, *"Tum dono ke paas ek-doosre ke liye koi pyaare nicknames hain kya? Jaise 'Saamu' aur 'Annie'?"* Ananya rolled her eyes, trying to hide her amusement. *"Tanya, tu bahut romantic filmein dekhti hai. Yahan Bollywood film nahi chal rahi. Hum sirf dost hain, main sach keh rahi hoon."*

Tanya leaned in, her tone conspiratorial. *"Arey bolo na, Ananya, kuch toh batao. Kya tumne koi 'accidental' hand grazes moments ya phir campaign ke kisi chandni raat mein koi lamha bitaya hai? Andheri raat aur sirf baat."* Ananya answered, *"You've got quite the imagination, Tanya. Koi chandni raat ya hand grazes moment's nahi hua. Hum sirf apne kaam par focused the."*

Tanya raised an eyebrow, her teasing tone unabated. *"'Hum', alright, alright, I'll stop with the playful teasing. But I have to admit, tumhe Sameer ke saath apni dosti mein itna excited dekhkar acha lag raha hai."*

Ananya smiled, her cheeks still slightly flushed. *"Yeh sach mein exciting hai, Tanya. He's an incredible person mein apni dosti ke liye grateful hoon. Lekin abhi ke liye, let's continue changing lives."*

As they continued their banter, Ananya couldn't help but appreciate Tanya's unwavering support and light-hearted teasing. While her friendship with Sameer was special, her bond with Tanya was equally cherished, and she knew she could always count on her friend to add some laughter and playfulness to her life.

Reunited by Serendipity

Years had passed since Sameer and Ananya's paths first crossed during their volunteer campaign in the rural village. Life had taken them on different journeys, but fate had other plans for them. One crisp autumn morning, their worlds would once again collide in the most unexpected way.

Sameer had embarked on a career in medicine, working diligently as a dedicated doctor. His days were filled with patients, medical rounds, and the constant pursuit of providing healthcare to those in need. However, amid the chaos of the hospital, his thoughts would often drift back to the days of volunteering in that remote village, where he had met Ananya.

Ananya, on the other hand, had continued to pursue her passion for poetry and social change. She had published her first poetry collection and had become an advocate for using art as a means to create a positive impact in the world. Her poetry resonated with people, inspiring them to reflect on the human condition and the power of empathy.

One evening, as Sameer was checking his emails, a familiar name appeared in his inbox – Ananya. It was a forwarded message from a colleague who had heard about Ananya's work and thought Sameer might be interested. The email contained an invitation to a poetry reading event in the city, where Ananya would be sharing her latest work.

Sameer couldn't believe his luck. He immediately replied, expressing his eagerness to attend the event. As the day of the poetry reading drew nearer, he couldn't help but feel a sense of anticipation and excitement.

The evening arrived, and Sameer found himself in a dimly lit café, the soft glow of string lights casting a warm ambiance. The room was filled with poetry enthusiasts and art lovers, all gathered to hear Ananya's words.

Ananya took the stage, her presence magnetic as she recited her verses, each word dripping with emotion. Her poetry delved into themes of love, compassion, and the profound impact of human connection – themes that resonated deeply with Sameer.

After the event, Sameer approached Ananya, feeling a bit nervous. *"Aapki poetry sachmuch bahut achi hoti hai."* he began. *"It's a testament to the power of art to inspire change."*

Ananya smiled warmly, recognizing him instantly. *"Sameer, kitne saalon baad! Mein yakeen nahi kar sakti ki hum phir se mile hain."*

They began to chat, exchanging stories of their journeys since their time in the village. Sameer shared the challenges and triumphs of his medical career, while Ananya spoke passionately about her poetry and advocacy work.

As they talked, they realized how much they still had in common – their love for literature, their shared values, and their desire to make the world a better place. They exchanged phone numbers, promising to keep in touch this time.

In the days that followed, Sameer and Ananya started texting regularly, sharing snippets of their daily lives, their thoughts on books and art, and their dreams for the future. Their friendship rekindled effortlessly, as if no time had passed at all.

Sameer would often send Ananya photos of the sunrise from the hospital rooftop, and Ananya would reply with verses inspired by those very images. They found solace in their conversations, their bond deepening with each passing day.

One sunny afternoon, as Sameer was on a break between appointments, he received a message from Ananya. It was a poem, *'Tum'* a beautiful tribute to their rekindled friendship and the serendipity that had brought them together once more.

Moved by her words, Sameer couldn't help but smile. He knew that this time, their connection was meant to endure – a testament to the enduring power of friendship and the beauty of unexpected reunions.

Friends and the Teasing Hearts

One sunny afternoon, Ananya decided it was time to introduce Sameer to her close friend, Tanya. She believed that Tanya's infectious energy and playful nature would make the introduction memorable, even though Ananya was insistent that there was nothing romantic between her and Sameer.

Ananya had arranged a casual get-together at a cozy cafe where they could all relax and chat. As they settled into their seats, Ananya couldn't help but feel a bit nervous about how the meeting would go.

"Sameer, this is Tanya," Ananya said, gesturing to her vivacious friend. *"Tanya, meet Sameer, my partner in our volunteer work."*

Tanya's eyes twinkled mischievously as she extended her hand to Sameer. *"Ah, so you're the famous 'Mr. Sameer', bahut suna hai Maine tumhare baare mein. Ananya har samay tumhare hi baare mein baat karti hai."*

Sameer smiled warmly, shaking Tanya's hand. *"Tum se mil kar khushi hui, 'Ms. Tanya.' Ananya ne bhi tumhare baare mein mujhe bahut kuch bataya hai."*

Tanya leaned in, her voice lighthearted. *"Oh, she has, has she? Don't worry; I promise not to reveal any embarrassing secrets... lekin agar tum chaho toh kuch masaledaar bachpan ki kahaniyan sunna chahte hain toh batao!"*

Ananya couldn't help but blush at Tanya's teasing. *"Tanya, don't you dare!"*

Sameer chuckled, already feeling at ease in Tanya's company. *"Mujhe lagta hai ki mein bhi woh kahaniya sunna pasand karunga, lekin chalo use kisi aur samay ke liye rakhte hain."*

Their meeting continued with laughter, friendly banter, and the exchange of stories. Tanya's teasing was relentless but good-natured, and Sameer handled it with grace and humor. It became evident that their camaraderie was natural, and the chemistry between the trios was undeniable.

They shared stories of their adventures during their recent healthcare campaign. Tanya, with her gift for storytelling, painted vivid pictures of their experiences, adding playful embellishments to keep them entertained.

Tanya leaned in closer to Ananya, her voice dropping to a conspiratorial whisper; *"Ananya, I have to say,"* Tanya began with a sly grin, *"Maine aaj tak tumko itne passionate nahi dekha kisi project ke liye. Kya tumhe nahi lagta hai ki isme kuch chupa hua hai, koi secret ingredient?"*

Tanya leaned forward, her curiosity piqued. *"Well, Sameer, Tum Ananya ke baare mein kya sochte hain? Kya woh is partnership mein utni hi dedicated hain jitne tum ho?"* Sameer chuckled, his warm eyes meeting Ananya's. *"Ananya is not just dedicated; she's incredibly passionate and driven. Ananya's dedication to our cause is truly inspiring, and I'm honored ki mein uske saath kaam kar raha hoon. Usmein dil me acchayi hai aur uska jazba bahut influence karne wala hai. Mujhe nahi lagta Hamare campaign ke liye inse behtar partner mujhe mil sakta tha"*

Sameer's phone chimed with a notification. He glanced at the screen and then at Ananya apologetically. *"Ananya, I'm really sorry, Lekin mujhe is call ko pick karna hoga."* Sameer explained his sense of responsibility evident in his voice. Ananya nodded understandingly. *"Of course, Sameer. tum call lo; Duty first."*

As he delved into the conversation on the phone, Sameer couldn't help but glance over at Ananya from time to time, a fond smile playing on his lips. He knew that their friendship was something truly special, and he was grateful for the moments they shared, whether in lively discussions or playful teasing.

Ananya chuckled softly, leaning in to respond to Tanya's whispered words, *"I know, Tanya, and I appreciate your curiosity. Just remember, jab bhi samay sahi hoga, tumhe sabse pehle pata chalega."* Tanya grinned mischievously, her secret-keeping abilities on full display. *"I'll hold you to that, Ananya. Until then, let's keep changing the lives."* Both laughed.

The evening continued with shared laughter, stories, and the promise of many more adventures together. Tanya's playful teasing persisted, but it only added to the warmth and joy of their friendship. It was a day that solidified the bond between Sameer, Ananya, and Tanya, reminding them that they were not just friends; they were a trio united by a shared purpose and a shared sense of humour.

Renewed Dreams

Sameer and Ananya's rekindled friendship blossomed with each passing day. They began to make an effort to meet in person whenever their busy schedules allowed, sharing moments of laughter, deep conversations, and a genuine connection that seemed to grow stronger with time.

One memorable weekend, they decided to embark on an impromptu road trip to a picturesque hill station they had both wanted to visit. As they drove through winding mountain roads, their favorite tunes playing in the background, they couldn't help but marvel at the serendipity that had brought them back into each other's lives.

During their hill station getaway, they explored quaint cafes, hiked to breathtaking viewpoints, and took long walks through lush forests. It was during one of these walks, as they stood on the edge of a cliff, gazing at the panoramic view of the valley below, that Ananya turned to Sameer with a twinkle in her eye.

"Sameer," she began, *"Kya tumhe yaad hai woh gaon jahan humne saath mein kaam kiya tha pehli baar?"*

Sameer nodded, his gaze fixed on the horizon. *"Of course, Mujhe yaad hai. It was a life-changing experience."*

Ananya smiled, her voice filled with nostalgia. *"Well, it got me thinking. What if hum ek naya village campaign shuru karein, iss baar kuch bada? Tumhari medical expertise hai aur meri advocacy work, isse hum aur bhi greater impact la sakte hain."*

Sameer turned to her, his eyes bright with enthusiasm. *"Ananya, that's an incredible idea! Let's do it. Saath milkar, hum sach mein ek difference bana sakte hain."*

Their decision to collaborate on a new campaign marked the beginning of a remarkable journey. Sameer and Ananya used their respective skills and networks to plan a healthcare initiative in an underserved region. They worked tirelessly, coordinating with medical teams, securing resources, and spreading the word about their mission.

Tanya's Touch of Magic in Their Journey

Tanya, their dear friend and confidante, was an integral part of Sameer and Ananya's journey. She had witnessed the evolution of their friendship and shared in their dreams of creating positive change in the world. When Sameer and Ananya approached her with their idea for a new healthcare campaign, Tanya didn't hesitate to join them.

Months passed, and the campaign came to fruition. They arrived at the same rural village where they had first met, but this time, they brought with them a larger team and a more extensive set of services. Sameer provided medical consultations and treatments, while Ananya used her platform to raise awareness about healthcare and hygiene.

Tanya brought her own unique skills to the table. With her background in communications and her knack for storytelling, she took charge of spreading the word about their mission. Through powerful narratives and compelling visuals, Tanya made sure their campaign resonated with a wider audience.

The impact they made was profound. The village, once plagued by preventable illnesses, began to see improvements in health and well-being. Sameer and Ananya's joint efforts not only changed lives but also inspired the villagers to take charge of their healthcare.

During the campaign, Tanya's presence was a source of encouragement and positivity. She engaged with the villagers, listened to their stories, and shared their experiences through her writing. Her ability to connect with people, combined with Sameer's medical expertise and Ananya's advocacy, created a holistic approach to healthcare and community empowerment.

As they wrapped up the campaign and prepared to return to their respective lives, Sameer and Ananya realized that their friendship had transformed into something even more profound. They had become partners in a mission to create positive change, their bond stronger than ever.

Their story was a testament to the enduring power of friendship, the magic of serendipity, and the profound impact two kindred spirits could have when they shared a common purpose. Sameer and Ananya continued their separate journeys, but they knew that no matter where life took them, their paths would always have a way of crossing, and their friendship would remain a source of inspiration and strength.

In the evenings, after a long day of work in the village, the trios sit around a campfire, sharing stories and laughter. Tanya's sense of humor and infectious laughter added a sense of warmth and camaraderie to their evenings. She would often tease Sameer and Ananya about their undeniable connection, despite their insistence that they were just friends. *"Chalo, tum dono,"* Tanya would say with a playful grin, *"Log tum dono ko ek couple samajhte hai iska koi karan to hai. Tum dono ek dynamic duo banate ho!"* Sameer and Ananya would exchange amused glances, knowing that Tanya's teasing was all in good spirits. They valued her friendship and the energy she brought to their shared mission.

The healthcare campaign was a resounding success, thanks to the combined efforts of Sameer, Ananya, and Tanya. They celebrated not only the tangible improvements in the village but also the strength of their friendship and their ability to come together to create meaningful change.

As they bid farewell to the villagers and returned to their everyday lives, Tanya continued to play an essential role in their friendship. She was the one who kept their connection alive, organizing regular meet-ups and ensuring that their bond remained as strong as ever.

In the end, Tanya, Sameer, and Ananya were more than just friends; they were a trio united by a shared purpose, unwavering support for each other, and a belief in the transformative power of friendship and collaboration. Together, they continued to inspire and uplift those around them, leaving a lasting impact on everyone they encountered.

A Clash of Intentions

After their delightful campaign, Sameer and Ananya found themselves excitedly planning their next get-together. Their shared love for literature had ignited a spark between them, and they couldn't wait to explore more bookstores and cafes in the city together.

However, as they began exchanging messages to arrange their next meeting, a misunderstanding started brewing. Ananya, always spontaneous and eager for adventure, suggested they meet at a quirky, offbeat café she had recently discovered. She thought it would be a fun surprise for Sameer.

Sameer, on the other hand, had already made plans to visit a traditional tea house he had read about in a book. He was looking forward to the tranquil atmosphere and the chance to try some unique teas. When he received Ananya's message about the café, he assumed she was suggesting it as a great place for their next meeting.

Unbeknownst to each other's intentions, Sameer and Ananya arrived at different locations that day. Ananya, excited to share her newfound spot, eagerly waited at the quirky café. Sameer, expecting to find Ananya there, was puzzled when he couldn't spot her in the bustling tea house.

Frustration and confusion mounted as they both tried calling and messaging each other, wondering why they couldn't locate each other. Sameer grew impatient, thinking that Ananya was late or had forgotten their plan. Ananya, on the other hand, started to feel anxious, fearing that Sameer had lost interest in their budding friendship.

Their misunderstandings intensified when they eventually met up, each feeling hurt and frustrated. Ananya, her eyes welled up with tears, said, *"Mujhe laga tumne mujhe akela chhod diya, Sameer. Main wahan cafe mein ghanto tak tumhara intezaar kar rahi thi!"*

Sameer, equally upset, replied, *"Maine socha tum wahan jana chahti ho. Mujhe nahi pata tha ki tum mera intezaar kar rahi thi. Mujhe lagta hai ki tumhe is baare mein koi fark nahi padta."*

Their emotions boiled over, and what started as a misunderstanding quickly escalated into a heated argument. Harsh words were exchanged, and both of them walked away, feeling hurt and misunderstood.

Days turned into weeks, and the silence between them grew deeper. They missed the connection they had felt during their campaign, but their wounded pride and stubbornness prevented them from reaching out to each other.

Reconciliation and Renewal

As the days passed, the rift between Sameer and Ananya grew wider. What had once been a blossoming friendship was now marred by bitterness and regret. They both missed the connection they had shared, but pride and stubbornness kept them from reaching out to each other.

The tension between Sameer and Ananya weighed heavily on both of them. Their once-thriving friendship had hit a rough patch due to the misunderstanding, and neither of them felt at peace with the way things had ended. Ananya couldn't help but replay the argument in her mind, feeling regret for not communicating her intentions more clearly. She missed the easy camaraderie they had shared during their campaigns and late-night chats. She realized that her spontaneous nature had inadvertently caused this rift, and she was determined to make amends.

On the other side of the city, Sameer found himself equally troubled by the fallout. He missed the warmth of Ananya's friendship and her infectious enthusiasm for life. He understood that his assumptions had played a part in their disagreement and wished he had taken a moment to clarify things before the situation escalated.

Tanya, who had been a silent observer of their growing bond, was deeply saddened by the turn of events. She couldn't bear to see her two friends at odds with each other, especially when their friendship had brought so much joy and inspiration to their lives.

One evening, Tanya decided to take matters into her own hands. She invited both Sameer and Ananya to a small gathering at her home, without revealing that the other would be there. Tanya hoped that in the comfort of her cozy living room, with a few friendly faces around, they might find a way to mend their broken friendship.

As Sameer and Ananya entered Tanya's home separately, they were greeted by warm smiles and the comforting aroma of freshly brewed tea. Tanya had set the perfect stage for reconciliation.

Sameer and Ananya's eyes met across the room, and for a moment, they couldn't look away. The memories of their shared adventures and heartfelt conversations flooded back. They both longed to bridge the gap that had grown between them.

Tanya, with her trademark intuition, sensed the unspoken tension. She began to steer the conversation toward their past campaigns, the lives they had touched, and the difference they had made together. It was a reminder of the beautiful synergy they had shared.

As the evening wore on, the walls they had built around their hearts began to crumble. Sameer, unable to contain his regret any longer, turned to Ananya and said, *"Ananya is misunderstanding ke liye main sach mein sorry. Mujhe behtar tarah se tumhe batna chahiye tha."*

Ananya, her eyes moist with emotion, replied, *"I'm sorry too, Sameer. I overreacted, mujhe tum par bharosa karna chahiye tha."*

Tanya smiled knowingly as she watched her friends clear the air and, in doing so; rekindle the special connection they had shared. Their apologies were met with understanding and forgiveness, and they both knew that their friendship was too precious to let go.

As the evening came to a close, they made plans for their next campaign, eager to channel their shared passions toward a common goal once more. This time, they had learned the importance of open communication and trust, two pillars that would strengthen their friendship in the face of future misunderstandings.

Sameer and Ananya understood that even the strongest friendships could face challenges but, with patience, understanding, and a little help from a caring friend like Tanya, they could emerge stronger than ever. Their friendship, once tested by a heated argument, emerged even stronger, and they continued their adventures in the world of books and beyond, cherishing the lessons they had learned about communication and forgiveness along the way.

Whispers among the Trees

S ameer and Ananya's love had blossomed over time, overcoming obstacles and misunderstandings that had initially threatened to pull them apart. Their bond had only grown stronger, and Sameer knew that he wanted to spend the rest of his life with Ananya. He decided to plan the perfect proposal to show her just how much she meant to him.

Sameer knew that Ananya had a deep love for nature and adventure, so he chose to propose in a place that held a special meaning for both of them— the serene forest where they had embarked on their first adventure together. It was a place where they had shared laughter, discovered hidden trails, and made beautiful memories.

One sunny afternoon, Sameer suggested they revisit the forest, reminiscing about their adventures. Ananya happily agreed, always eager for a day of exploration and adventure.

As they wandered through the forest, Sameer carefully planned each step of the proposal. He had enlisted the help of a close friend who was a talented photographer to capture the moment. The friend discreetly followed them, camera in hand, ready to document this special occasion.

Sameer led Ananya to a picturesque clearing in the forest, bathed in dappled sunlight. The gentle rustling of leaves and the melody of birds provided the perfect backdrop. Ananya, caught up in the beauty of the moment, didn't suspect what was about to happen.

Sameer turned to Ananya, his eyes filled with love and sincerity. *"Ananya,"* he began, his voice trembling with emotion, *"Jabse maine uss campaign mein tumse milkar tumhe jana, tabse meri zindagi badal gayi hai. Tumne mere dinon ko hansne, sair karne, aur pyaar se bhar diya hai. Mai ek bhi din imagine nahi kar sakta, jab tum mere paas na ho."*

Ananya's eyes widened in surprise, realizing that this wasn't an ordinary forest adventure. Sameer continued, *"Har din tumhare saath ek incredible journey rahi hai, aur mai chahta hoon ki yeh hamesha aise hi chalti rahe. Kya tum mujhe duniya ka sabse khush insan banoge; Will you marry me?"*

As he spoke these heartfelt words, Sameer knelt down on one knee, lifted Ananya's foot, and placed a stunning toe ring that sparkled in the gentle sunlight. Ananya's heart soared with happiness and surprise as tears welled up in her eyes.

"Yes, yes, a thousand times yes!" Ananya exclaimed, her voice trembling with joy. She reached out to embrace Sameer, sealing their commitment with a loving cheek kiss.

Their friend, the photographer, captured the entire moment, freezing in time the love and happiness that radiated from the newly engaged couple.

In the midst of nature's beauty, surrounded by the echoes of their shared adventures, Sameer and Ananya began a new chapter of their love story.

Their proposal in the forest was a testament to the depth of their connection and the adventures they would continue to share for the rest of their lives.

Coffee, Conversations, and Wedding Dreams

After the enchanting forest proposal, Ananya couldn't wait to share the exciting news with her close friend Tanya. She arranged a cozy meet up at their favorite café, where the scent of freshly brewed coffee always added warmth to their conversations.

As Ananya settled into her chair across from Tanya, she couldn't contain her excitement. *"Tanya, you won't believe what happened!"* she began, her eyes sparkling with joy.

Tanya leaned in eagerly. *"Sab kuch batao, Ananya. Tum bilkul excited lag rahi ho, mujhe sab sunna hai."*

With a wide smile, Ananya recounted the forest proposal, painting a vivid picture of the sun-dappled clearing, Sameer's heartfelt words, and the sparkling ring that had sealed their commitment. Tanya listened intently, her eyes filled with happiness for her dear friend.

"Oh, Ananya, yeh toh bilkul magical lagta hai!" Tanya exclaimed when Ananya finished her tale. *"Main tumhare liye bahut khush hoon. Aur, Sameer toh sach mein bahut romantic hai, na?"*

Ananya nodded, her heart brimming with love. *"Woh bilkul hai. Aur sabse achhi baat yeh hai ki yeh usi jungle mein hua jahan humara adventure shuru hua tha. Yeh ek perfect full-circle moment tha."*

Tanya grinned mischievously. *"So, when's the big day? Shaadi ki planning shuru kar di hai kya?"*

Ananya chuckled. *"Nahi abhi, Tanya. Abhi toh hum is khoobsurat pal ko mahsoos kar rahe hain. Lekin kaun jane, shayad jaldi hi hum shaadi ki planning ke baare mein sochne lag jaayein."*

Tanya leaned back in her chair, her teasing tone returning. *"Achha, jab tum log karoge, toh yaad rakhna, main ek bharosa wali wedding planner banungi, thik hai? Mere paas romantic aur nature-inspired wedding ke liye bahut saare ideas hain!"*

Ananya laughed, appreciating Tanya's enthusiasm. *"Main woh yaad rakhoongi, Tanya. Tere creative ideas hamare special din ko aur bhi khas bana denge."*

As they chatted about the proposal and their shared dreams for the future, Ananya couldn't help but feel grateful for Tanya's unwavering friendship. Tanya had been there through every twist and turn of her journey, offering support, laughter, and now, the promise of future wedding planning adventures.

The two friends continued to savor their coffee and each other's company, knowing that their friendship was a treasure to be cherished just as much as the love that had brought Ananya and Sameer together.

Under the Starry Canopy: A Proposal to Remember

As night fell and the stars began to twinkle in the vast sky, Sameer and Ananya found themselves engaged in a quiet yet deeply meaningful conversation. The forest proposal was still fresh in their minds, and its magic seemed to linger in the air.

Sameer, his voice soft and filled with affection, spoke first. *"Ananya tonight has been one of the most beautiful moments of my life. Seeing your eyes light up when I proposed in that forest, it's a memory I'll cherish forever."*

Ananya smiled, her heart dancing with happiness. *"Sameer, it was beyond perfect. You've made me the happiest person in the world."*

They fell into a comfortable silence, the night around them hushed and serene. The gentle rustling of leaves and the distant chirping of crickets provided a soothing soundtrack to their conversation.

Sameer reached for Ananya's hand, their fingers intertwining. *"Ananya, I promise to love you with all my heart, to be your partner in adventure, and to cherish every moment we share. Together, there's nothing we can't overcome."*

Ananya's eyes glistened with emotion as she whispered, *"Sameer, I promise to stand by your side, to love you fiercely, and to create a life filled with love, laughter, and beautiful adventures."*

Ananya, her voice filled with curiosity, asked Sameer, *"Do you remember the first book we bonded over at the bookstore?"* Sameer chuckled softly, his thumb gently tracing circles on the back of Ananya's hand. *"Of course, I do. It was 'Anjanne Ajnabee' by Aayush Maatrishya. I still remember how your eyes lit up when you mentioned it."*

Ananya, her voice carrying a thoughtful tone, remarked, *"You know, 'Anjanne Ajnabee' teaches us so much about unspoken bonds and unresolved emotions. It's incredible how the characters in the story navigate their complex relationships."*

Sameer nodded, his eyes reflecting the starlight above. *"Absolutely, Ananya. The unspoken words, the hidden feelings—it's a reflection of real life, isn't it? Sometimes, the most profound connections are those that remain unspoken."*

Sameer asked, *"Acha, what are your thoughts about the characters?"*

Ananya answered, *"Hmm... Maatrishya to swam prem ke rachyeta hai to, wo sirf prem ki baat karenge, nischal aur niswarth prem. Lekin agar sansar ki drishti se dekhe to bina naam diye prem pura hi nahi hai, to mujhe lagta hai Maatrishya use dost ya hai bhai-behen ka naam denge."*

"Mujhe bhi yahi lagta hai," Sameer replied.

Ananya asked, *"Lekin mujhe ek baat samajh nahi aayi ki Maatrishya puri kahani mein hai kahan?"*

Sameer replied, *"Iska jawab to unhonne Maatrishya Uvach ke akhiri paragraph me diya hai, 'What happens next, only two people know. One is me, and the other is time. I won't reveal it because my job is not to predict the future, and as for time, it is ready to tell, but it hasn't arrived yet. **'Some might wonder where I am, so let me clarify, I am Sarvvyapi.'** to wo hai kahan wo sirf wahi jante hai, aur unka samay janta hai."*

As they delved deeper into the intricacies of the characters and their relationships, Ananya and Sameer found themselves not just analyzing a story but also reflecting on their own lives, the unspoken bonds they shared, and the growth they had experienced together.

Ananya said, *"Tumhe nahi lagta hai ki kaise hum campaign mein mile phir bookstore, aur phir humari fight bhi hui, lekin we understood the importance of open communication, and the demerits of unspoken feelings"*

Sameer smiled, his fingers gently intertwining with Ananya's. *"Tum sahi keh rahi ho, Ananya. Yeh aisa lagta hai jaise ki universe ne humari kahani ko pehle hi likh diya hai, aur hum uske likhe hue script ko bas follow kar rahe the."*

Their foreheads gently touched as they closed their eyes, savoring the depth of their connection. In that quiet moment beneath the starlit sky, Sameer and Ananya knew that their love was a force of nature, unshakable and enduring.

As the night continued to weave its tapestry of stars, they whispered sweet nothings, sharing their dreams and desires. The forest around them seemed to hold its breath, honoring the love that had blossomed within its depths.

For Sameer and Ananya, every moment together was a page in their love story, and they were excited to fill it with the most beautiful adventures life had to offer.

Moonlit Conversations

As Sameer and Ananya shared their dreams and aspirations, the night seemed to cocoon them in a world of possibilities. Their conversation meandered through the realms of literature, medicine, poetry, and travel, creating an intricate tapestry of shared interests and ambitions.

Ananya, her eyes filled with curiosity, asked, *"Sameer, what made you decide to become a doctor?"* Sameer leaned back against the park bench, reminiscing about his journey. *"Well, it all started with my nanaji. He was a physician, and his stories of helping people, of making a real difference in their lives, left a profound impact on me. I wanted to follow in his footsteps, to carry forward his legacy of compassion and service."*

Ananya's admiration for him shone through as she responded, *"That's beautiful, Sameer. Your dedication to helping others is truly inspiring."*

Sameer smiled, grateful for her understanding. *"And what about you, Ananya? What inspired you to become a poet?"* Ananya's gaze turned introspective. *"For me, it was the power of words. I believe that poetry has the ability to touch hearts, to inspire change, and to express the deepest of emotions. I wanted to use my words to make a positive impact on the world, to create a space where people could find solace and understanding."* Sameer nodded in appreciation. *"You do that beautifully, Ananya. Your poetry has touched my heart many times."*

Ananya's eyes sparkled with enthusiasm as she spoke about her dream project, a poetry anthology that aimed to amplify the voices of marginalized communities. *"I want to use the power of poetry to shed light on the stories and struggles of those often unheard,"* she explained.

Sameer was captivated by her passion. *"That's incredible, Ananya. I'll be there to support you every step of the way."*

Their exchange was peppered with laughter, with Sameer occasionally sharing funny anecdotes from his experiences as a doctor, and Ananya recounting amusing encounters during her poetry readings.

But it wasn't all lighthearted banter. At times, they delved into deeper conversations about life's challenges and the importance of resilience. Ananya admired Sameer's unwavering commitment to his patients, and Sameer found solace in Ananya's ability to find beauty and meaning even in the most difficult of situations.

They were still holding hands. The moon cast a gentle glow upon them as they shared more intimate details about their lives. Ananya revealed the story behind her favorite poem, a piece that had been inspired by a childhood memory of her grandmother. Sameer listened intently, his eyes never leaving Ananya's face. *"Your ability to capture such depth of emotion in your words is truly a gift,"* he remarked.

Ananya blushed, grateful for his encouragement. *"And you, Sameer, your dedication to saving lives and making a difference in this world is inspiring. I've seen your compassion firsthand during our campaigns."*

As the night wore on, they talked about their families, their dreams of traveling the world, and the simple pleasures they cherished. The unspoken bond between them seemed to deepen with each word exchanged.

As the clock ticked on, Sameer couldn't help but be grateful for the unspoken bond they shared. He realized that love wasn't just about grand gestures or extravagant proposals; it was about these quiet moments, where their hearts and souls connected, where they shared their dreams, and where they found solace in each other's presence.

Sameer's phone chimed with a notification. He looked at Ananya, his eyes filled with warmth. *"It's getting late, Ananya. We should head back."*

Ananya nodded, a soft smile gracing her lips. *"Thank you for tonight, Sameer. It was perfect."*

As they finally made their way back to their cars, Sameer couldn't help but feel that this night had been truly magical. He looked at Ananya and said, *"Ananya, I cherish our time together, whether it's under the sun or beneath the stars. You bring so much light into my life."* Ananya smiled, her heart filled with warmth. *"Sameer, you've become an irreplaceable part of my world. I can't wait to see where our journey takes us next."*

Hand in hand, they walked back through the park, their hearts light, knowing that their unspoken bond was stronger than ever, and their love would continue to grow, nurturing their dreams and aspirations in the embrace of each other's company.

The Enchanted Rainforest: A Journey of Discovery

PAUSE THE WHOLE SCENARIO *"Love undergoes many tests, not to prove that you have true love, but because it makes the bonds of love unbreakable. It's in facing these trials together that love becomes stronger and more enduring. Just as a tree's roots grow deeper during storms, love too deepens through life's challenges, becoming a source of strength and resilience. These tests of love are not meant to break us but to shape us, to transform us into better versions of ourselves, capable of loving more deeply and unconditionally.*

So, as Sameer and Ananya continue on their journey together, let's see what challenges and adventures lay ahead. Perhaps they will encounter obstacles that test their patience, misunderstandings that challenge their communication, or external pressures that put their relationship to the test. But one thing is certain, their love, like a diamond forged under pressure, will shine even brighter if it withstands these trials. Together, they will learn that love is not just a feeling; it's a commitment, a partnership, and a journey that they are willing to embark on, hand in hand, no matter what comes their way."

Ananya's passion for exploring new cultures, tasting exotic cuisines, and immersing herself in the local way of life was the driving force behind her successful career.

One day, Ananya received an intriguing assignment from a prestigious travel magazine. She was tasked with venturing into the heart of the Amazon Rainforest, an enchanting yet perilous destination. The goal was to document the lives of indigenous tribes living deep within the jungle and to shed light on their unique customs, traditions, and the challenges they faced due to environmental changes.

Thrilled about this exciting opportunity to embark on a transformative journey, Ananya called Sameer and shared the news. He couldn't have been happier for her, knowing that this experience would bring about a significant change in her career. He reassured her of his unwavering support and promised to be by her side, even if it meant they would be physically apart for a while.

Ananya also made a call to Tanya, her close friend, to share the news. Tanya's excitement matched Ananya's, and she expressed how proud she was of her friend for seizing this opportunity.

With her bags packed, including her trusty notebook and camera, Ananya set off for the Amazon. She understood that this adventure would test her limits, both physically and creatively, but she was determined to bring the world a glimpse of the mesmerizing beauty hidden within the lush rainforest.

As she boarded the plane, she couldn't help but feel a rush of anticipation for the incredible journey that awaited her, knowing that her bonds with Sameer and Tanya would remain strong, no matter the distance.

As she ventured deeper into the Amazon, Ananya was welcomed by the warmth and curiosity of the indigenous tribes. She spent her days learning their ancient practices, from traditional medicine to hunting techniques. Nights were filled with stories around the campfire, with the stars overhead and the symphony of the jungle as her background music.

Throughout her journey, Ananya discovered that the Amazon was not only a place of unparalleled biodiversity but also a realm of deep connection between its inhabitants and the natural world. The tribes she encountered had a profound understanding of their ecosystem and a profound respect for the delicate balance of life within it.

Ananya's writing came alive as she eloquently portrayed the vibrant tapestry of cultures she encountered. Her stories spoke of resilience, the celebration of life's simple pleasures, and the looming threats that deforestation posed to these ancient tribes and their way of life.

Back home, as she crafted her articles and edited her photographs, Ananya felt a deep sense of responsibility to raise awareness about the preservation of the Amazon Rainforest. Her writing became a powerful tool for advocating for sustainable practices and the protection of these remote communities.

Her work earned her accolades and recognition from both readers and environmental organizations. Ananya's articles were instrumental in sparking discussions about the urgent need to conserve the Amazon, not just for its unparalleled biodiversity but also for the preservation of cultures and traditions that had thrived for centuries.

Ananya's journey into the Amazon was more than just an assignment; it was a life-changing experience that allowed her to use her passion for travel writing to make a difference in the world. Her stories served as a testament to the unbreakable bonds between humanity and nature, and her commitment to their preservation became her life's mission.

Distance and Teasing

In the heart of the Amazon Rainforest, surrounded by the lush green canopy and the symphony of wildlife, Ananya had immersed herself in documenting the lives of indigenous tribes. Her days were filled with learning their customs and traditions, while her nights were spent by the campfire, listening to their stories under the starlit sky.

Back in the city, Sameer and Tanya eagerly awaited her return. They had missed Ananya more than they could put into words. Sameer's phone chimed with a message, and his face lit up as he read Ananya's name.

"She messaged!" Sameer exclaimed to Tanya, his voice filled with excitement.

Tanya, with a sly grin, leaned over to look at the message. *"Well, don't keep us in suspense. What's the latest from the Amazon?"*

Sameer read the message aloud, *"Hey, you two! I can't wait to share all the incredible stories and experiences I've had here. It's been eye-opening and challenging in so many ways, but I love every moment. I hope you're both doing well!"*

Tanya couldn't resist teasing Sameer. *"Aww, Sameer, it sounds like she's having a blast. But it also sounds like she's missing us."*

Sameer chuckled, knowing that Tanya was right. *"You might be onto something, Tanya. She's probably missing our late-night conversations and her teasing sessions."*

Tanya grinned mischievously. *"You know, Sameer, maybe we should send her a selfie together, just to remind her of what she's missing."*

Sameer raised an eyebrow, playing along. *"Oh, I see where you're going with this, Tanya. Let's do it."*

They snapped a quick selfie, with Tanya holding the camera and Sameer making a goofy face. Tanya added a playful caption: *"Wish you were here, Ananya! Sameer and I are having so much fun without you."*

Sameer laughed as Tanya hit send. *"That should get her attention."*

Sure enough, within minutes, Ananya responded with a laughing emoji and a message: *"You two are impossible! I miss you both more than words can express. Don't have too much fun without me!"*

Tanya winked at Sameer. *"See, I told you she was missing us."*

Tanya couldn't resist a playful jab. *"So Sameer how's life without Ananya around? Lonely, isn't it?"*

Sameer chuckled, used to Tanya's good-natured teasing. *"Well, it's definitely quieter without her, but I'm managing just fine."*

Tanya gave him a mischievous grin. *"Oh, come on, Sameer. Admit it, you miss her. You miss her poetic ramblings and her endless enthusiasm for trying new things."*

Sameer nodded, unable to deny it. *"You're right, Tanya. I do miss her. Her presence always brightens up my day."*

Tanya decided to take it a step further. *"And how about those late-night conversations you two used to have? Deep, soul-searching talks about the meaning of life and the mysteries of the universe."*

Sameer chuckled. *"Okay, I'll admit it. Those late-night conversations were something special. Ananya has a unique way of making you see things from a different perspective."*

Tanya changed her tone conspiratorial. *"You know, Sameer, I think you secretly enjoy those conversations more than you let on. Maybe you even miss them more than you miss her."*

Sameer laughed, realizing that Tanya had him cornered. *"Alright, alright, you got me. I miss both Ananya and our late-night talks. But don't tell her I said that."*

Tanya winked. *"Your secret's safe with me, Mr. Sameer. Just remember, absence makes the heart grow fonder."*

Sameer couldn't help but smile at his friend's playful teasing. Despite the distance, Tanya's friendship and banter were a source of comfort and laughter during Ananya's absence, reinforcing the knowledge that the bond between Ananya and him and their cherished friendship remained as strong as ever.

Ananya's Return

After several months of immersing herself in the mesmerizing world of the Amazon Rainforest, Ananya to her bustling city, a place where the rhythms of life were as different as night and day compared to the jungle. The transition was both exhilarating and overwhelming.

As she stepped off the plane, Ananya felt a rush of emotions. The concrete jungle that greeted her was a stark contrast to the lush green canopy of the Amazon. The cacophony of the city, with its honking cars and bustling crowds, was a far cry from the serene symphony of the rainforest.

Ananya carried with her a treasure trove of memories, experiences, and stories from her time in the Amazon. Her trusty notebook and camera were filled with images and notes that would soon find their way into her travel articles, each one a testament to the beauty and fragility of the natural world and the resilience of the indigenous tribes.

She couldn't wait to reunite with her close friend, Tanya, who had eagerly awaited her return. Tanya had followed Ananya's journey through their late-night chats and phone calls, sharing in her adventures and discoveries from afar. Now, she was excited to hear Ananya's stories in person.

Ananya's first stop was a quaint café, a place where she and Tanya had spent countless hours chatting and sipping chai. As she entered, Tanya spotted her from a distance and rushed over, enveloping her friend in a warm hug.

"Welcome back! Ananya" Tanya exclaimed. *"I've missed you so much. Tell me everything about your Amazon adventure."*

Over cups of steaming chai, Ananya regaled Tanya with tales of the rainforest, from her encounters with indigenous tribes to the breathtaking sights and sounds of nature's sanctuary. Tanya listened with rapt attention, hanging on to every word, her eyes sparkling with fascination.

But amid the tales of beauty and wonder, Ananya also shared the challenges faced by the Amazon Rainforest and its inhabitants. She spoke passionately about the urgent need for conservation and the importance of respecting indigenous cultures and their rights.

Tanya was moved by Ananya's dedication and determination to make a difference. *"Ananya, you've not only experienced something incredible but also used your talents to raise awareness,"* Tanya said. *"Your stories have the power to inspire change."*

As they continued to chat, Ananya couldn't help but feel grateful for her friend's unwavering support. Her return to the city marked a new chapter in her journey, one where she would use her experiences to advocate for the preservation of the Amazon Rainforest and its irreplaceable wonders.

Ananya was no longer just a travel writer; she had become a voice for nature and a champion for the people of the rainforest. Her stories would serve as a bridge between the urban world and the untouched wilderness, a reminder that even in the heart of the city, the call of the wild could be heard, and the bonds with nature remained unbreakable.

Reunion of Hearts

After reuniting with her close friend Tanya and sharing her Amazon adventure stories, Ananya couldn't wait to see Sameer, the person who had been a constant source of support and inspiration throughout her journey. Their bond had grown stronger over time, despite the physical distance that had separated them.

Ananya called Sameer, and they made plans to meet at their favorite park. As she arrived at the park, Ananya felt a sense of excitement mixed with anticipation. She spotted Sameer sitting on a bench under the shade of a towering oak tree, a warm smile on his face as he looked up to greet her.

"Ananya," Sameer said, standing up to embrace her, *"it's so good to see you again."*

Ananya returned the hug, her heart filled with warmth. *"Sameer, I've missed you so much. It feels like a lifetime since we last saw each other."*

They settled on the bench, catching up on the time they had spent apart. Ananya shared more about her experiences in the Amazon, the challenges she had faced, and the profound impact the journey had on her.

"I can't believe how much you've accomplished, Ananya," Sameer said, his admiration evident in his eyes. *"Your dedication to conservation and advocacy is truly inspiring."*

Ananya smiled, her gaze meeting Sameer's. *"I couldn't have done it without your support, Sameer. You've been my anchor, even from afar."*

As they sat there, the conversation shifted to lighter topics, and the familiar banter and playful teasing returned. Ananya couldn't help but feel a sense of completeness being in Sameer's company again.

"You know," Sameer began, his voice soft, *"I missed our late-night conversations and the way you'd share your thoughts and dreams with me."*

Ananya nodded, her heart fluttering. *"I missed them too, Sameer. There's something about talking to you that makes me feel like I'm truly understood."*

The sun began to set, casting a warm, and golden glow over the park. Sameer turned to Ananya, his expression tender. *"Ananya, there's something I want to say. This time apart made me realize just how much you mean to me. I missed you in ways I never thought possible."*

Ananya's heart skipped a beat as she looked into Sameer's eyes, seeing the sincerity and vulnerability in his gaze. *"Sameer,"* she replied, her voice soft and earnest, *"I missed you too, more than words can express. You're not just my friend; you're a part of my heart."*

In that moment, with the sun setting behind them and the park bathed in a warm, romantic glow, Ananya leaned in and gently kissed Sameer. It was a kiss that spoke of missed moments, unspoken feelings, and the depth of their connection.

As they pulled away, their foreheads touching, Sameer whispered, *"Ananya, I don't want to be apart from you anymore. I want to be with you, to share every moment, and to be by your side."*

Ananya smiled, her eyes shimmering with emotion. *"Sameer, I feel the same way. I've missed you every day, and I want nothing more than to be with you."*

Their reunion marked a new chapter in their relationship, one where they would no longer let distance keep them apart. It was a testament to the unspoken bonds and unresolved emotions that had grown between them, now finding expression in the embrace of a warm summer evening.

Bittersweet Farewell

Ananya's articles and photographs had not only earned her acclaim in the world of travel writing but had also ignited a passion for environmental advocacy. She was determined to continue raising awareness about the importance of preserving the world's most precious ecosystems.

However, life had a twist in store for Ananya. Just when she thought she was settled back into her routine, an unexpected career opportunity came knocking. An international magazine, impressed by her work on the Amazon, offered her a coveted position as a senior correspondent based in another city known for its rich cultural heritage and vibrant arts scene.

Ananya was faced with a difficult decision. The opportunity was a dream comes true for her career, but it meant leaving behind the city she had called home for years, as well as the close bonds she had nurtured with Sameer and Tanya.

She called Sameer to share the news, her voice tinged with both excitement and uncertainty. *"Sameer, ek amazing opportunity aayi hai mere career ke liye. Magar mujhe dusre city shift hona parega. Aur iska matlab hai ki hum phir se dur ho jayenge. Yeh kabhi nahi socha tha maine, aur mujhe samajh nahi aa raha kya karun."*

Sameer listened attentively, understanding the significance of the decision Ananya was facing. *"Ananya, mein jaanta hoon ki tumhara career tumhare liye kitna important hai, aur yeh opportunity tumhare liye ek kadam aage badhne ka mauka ho sakta hai. Humne pehle bhi long-distance relationship ka samna kiya hai, aur hum is baar bhi kar sakte hain. Tumhara har decision mein support karunga, chahe jo bhi tum faisla lo."*

Ananya also called Tanya, who offered her unwavering encouragement. *"Ananya, yeh ek aisi opportunity hai jo ek baar hi milti hai, aur tumne iske liye bahut mehnat ki hai. Change se darne se peechhe nahi hatna chahiye. Hume yahaan tumhari yaad aayegi, lekin hum hamesha ek phone call hi to door honge."*

As the day of Ananya's departure drew near, a palpable sense of sadness hung in the air. The thought of being separated once again weighed heavily on both Sameer and Ananya's hearts.

Sameer: (with a hint of melancholy) *"Ananya, mein khud ko rok nahi sakta. Humne isse pehle bhi face kiya hai, lekin yeh asaan nahi hota."*

Ananya: (softly) *"Pata hai, Sameer. Tumhari yaad aayegi mujhe, bahut yaad aayegi. Tumhare saath bitaye hue lamhe ne mere zindagi ke sabse yaadgar pal diye hain."*

Sameer: *"Aur mere liye bhi, Ananya. Tumne hi mere jeevan mein khushiyan bhari hain. Main nahi soch sakta ki tum mere liye bas ek phone call door ho."*

Ananya: (her voice tinged with emotion) *"Yeh goodbye nahi hai, Sameer. Yeh toh bas 'come back soon' hai. Hum jude rahenge, aur main vaada karti hoon ki hum ek-doosre se jitni baar bhi mil sakte hain, milenge."*

Sameer: (smiling through the sadness) *"Tum sahi keh rahi ho, Ananya. Duri humare rishte ko tootne nahi degi. Hum duriyon ko paar karne ke tarike nikal lenge, jaise hum hamesha karte hain."*

Tears welled up in Ananya's eyes as she hugged Sameer tightly. Their farewell was filled with a mixture of emotions – sadness at the prospect of being apart, but also hope and determination to make their friendship endure the test of distance once again.

As Ananya boarded the plane to her new city, she carried with her the memories of their shared adventures, the echoes of their laughter, and the warmth of their friendship. The sadness of parting was real, but so was the unwavering belief that their deep connection would keep them close.

Love's Distant Embrace

Ananya had finally settled into her new city, and her career as a travel writer was soaring to new heights. She had explored the vibrant culture, tasted delectable cuisines, and connected with local communities in ways she had never imagined. Yet, amidst the bustling cityscape and the excitement of new experiences, there was emptiness in her heart that only one person could fill.

One evening, as the city lights glittered below her window, Ananya decided to make a phone call that had been long overdue. She dialed Sameer's number and waited with bated breath for him to pick up.

After a few rings, Sameer's warm voice filled her ears, *"Hello?"*

Ananya's heart skipped a beat at the sound of his voice, and she couldn't help but smile. *"Hey, Saameer, it's me."*

Saameer's tone turned affectionate, *"Ananya, it's so good to hear your voice. Kaisi chal rahi hai nayi city?"*

Ananya couldn't contain the sadness that had been gnawing at her. *"Bohot mast, Saameer. Par ek baat yaad aa rahi hai... main tumhe miss kar rahi hoon."*

Saameer's voice held a hint of melancholy too, *"Main bhi tumhe miss kar raha hoon, Ananya. Tumhare bina yahan sab kuch adhoora sa lagta hai."*

Ananya sighed, her heart aching with longing. *"Pata hai, Saameer. Yeh city ki raat ki roshni toh khoobsurat hai, but they can't compare to the warmth of your smile."*

Saameer chuckled softly, *"And these city streets are bustling, but they can't replace the comfort of our shared laughter."*

As the conversation continued, they talked about their day-to-day lives, the small joys, and the challenges they faced. They shared stories of their respective cities, exchanging details about the sights and sounds that made their worlds unique.

Ananya couldn't help but express her feelings, *"Saameer, mujhe aisa lagta hai ki kuch kami hai yahan. Yeh city toh amazing hai, par tum mere saath nahi ho toh, kuch adhoora sa lagta hai."*

Saameer's voice softened, *"Ananya, doori humare pyaar ko kam nahi kar sakti. Hamara rishta bahut gehra hai, jo sirf physical presence se nahi juda hai. Humare pyaar mein, koi bhi daraar nahi aa sakti."*

Ananya wiped away a tear that had escaped her eye, her voice filled with emotion, *"Main jaanti hoon, Saameer. Bas... mein chahati hoon ki tum mere saath hote."*

Saameer's response was filled with longing, *"Main bhi chahata hoon ki mein tumhare saath hota, Ananya."*

Their conversation continued late into the night, with both of them finding solace in each other's words. The miles between them seemed insignificant as they shared their dreams, their hopes, and their love.

As they finally said their goodnights, Ananya whispered, *"Saameer, I love you."*

Saameer replied with equal fervor, *"I love you too, Ananya, more than words can express."*

Despite the distance that separated them, their love remained as strong as ever. Ananya closed her eyes, feeling the warmth of Saameer's love wrap around her like a comforting embrace, knowing that they would always find a way to bridge the gap between them.

A Proposal across the Miles

Ananya had been in a long-distance relationship with Saameer for quite some time now, and while their love was unwavering, the distance had started to take its toll on her. She missed him more than words could express, and the frustration of not being able to be with him was building up.

One evening, as they were on a video call, Ananya couldn't hold back her feelings any longer. She looked into Saameer's eyes through the screen and took a deep breath.

"Saameer," she began, her voice trembling with emotion, *"I can't do this anymore. I can't stand being so far away from you."*

Saameer, sensing her frustration and sadness, responded with concern, *"I know it's tough, Ananya, but we've been through this before, and we've always found a way."*

Ananya nodded, tears welling up in her eyes, *"Haan, Saameer, par ab aur nahi. Main chahti hoon hum saath ho. Main chahti hoon hum ek saath zindagi banaye."*

Saameer's eyes widened in surprise, *"Kya keh rahi ho, Ananya?"*

Ananya took a deep breath, her heart pounding with nervousness, *"Saameer, kya tum mujhse shaadi karoge?"*

Silence hung in the air as Saameer processed her words. Then, a slow smile spread across his face, and his eyes glistened with happiness.

"Yes, Ananya," he replied, his voice filled with love and excitement, *"I've been waiting for this moment. I want to marry you more than anything in the world."*

Ananya's face lit up with joy as they both realized that the frustration of distance had led to a life-changing decision. Their love had overcome the challenges of long-distance, and now they were taking the next step in their journey together. Ananya couldn't help but feel a profound sense of relief and happiness as they talked about their future, one where they would no longer be separated by miles, but instead, united in love and marriage.

Love Beyond Tradition

As Ananya returned to her family's home after a long absence, she couldn't help but feel a sense of anxiety. Ananya's father, Mr. Kumar, was a stern and traditional man who placed a high value on their family's culture and traditions. He was often seen as the head of the family and was deeply rooted in their conservative beliefs. Ananya's mother, Mrs. Kumar, was a caring and protective woman who supported her husband's traditional views wholeheartedly. She often played the role of a mediator between her husband's sternness and her daughters' desires.

Kajal, Ananya's younger sister, was now studying in the 10th standard. She was a bright and diligent student, always striving for academic excellence. Her worldview was largely influenced by her parents' beliefs and values, and she often looked up to her older sister Ananya as a role model.

Ananya knew that the news she was about to share would be met with even greater resistance from her family. The weight of their expectations, the clash between tradition and her love for Saameer, and the desire to bridge the gap between these two worlds weighed heavily on her heart. She understood that her journey ahead was fraught with challenges and the most dramatic and challenging moments of her life were yet to come.

During dinner that evening, Ananya finally mustered the courage to speak. *"Maa, Papa, I've got something important to share,"* she began.

Her parents exchanged knowing glances, sensing that this wasn't an ordinary conversation. Her father gestured for her to continue.

"Main kisi se pyaar karti hoon," Ananya said, her voice trembling slightly. *"Uska naam, Saameer hai."*

A heavy silence filled the room. Ananya's mother, her face etched with concern, finally spoke. *"Ananya, yeh kaisi baatein kar rahi ho? Tumhe toh pata hai hamare parivaar mein humare kitni izzat hai."*

Ananya's father, stern and unyielding, added, *"Hamare parivaar mein love marriage ke liye koi jagah nahi hai. Yeh galat hai, aur hum aise family traditions and culture bardasht nahi karte."*

As the tension in the room escalated, Ananya's father, unable to accept her revelation, abruptly left the table, leaving her mother deeply concerned and conflicted.

Tears welled up in Ananya's eyes as she tried to explain her feelings. *"Maa, mein jaanti hoon aapke liye family traditions and culture kitni importance rakhti hain, lekin mere liye bhi pyaar aur mere bhavishya ka haq hai."*

The conversation continued late into the night, with emotions running high. Ananya knew that this revelation had created a deep divide within her family, and the clash between tradition and her love for Saameer was tearing her apart.

The situation in Ananya's family continued to grow more complicated as the days passed. Her parents, staunch believers in tradition and arranged marriages, were deeply opposed to the idea of a love marriage. The atmosphere at home became increasingly tense, and arguments were a regular occurrence.

One evening, Ananya's mother, Shalini, approached her with tears in her eyes. *"Ananya, yeh tumhare liye nahi hai, humare liye hai. Tum samajh nahi sakti hamari parivaar ki maryada aur izzat kitni ahmiyat rakhti hai. Vada kar ki tu Saameer se kabhi nahi milegi, kabhi baat nahi karegi."*

Ananya was torn between her love for Saameer and her respect for her family's values. She knew that keeping such a promise would mean sacrificing her own happiness, but she also couldn't bear the thought of causing more pain to her parents.

The clash between tradition and her love for Saameer was tearing her apart, and the pressure from her family was relentless. Ananya's younger sister, Kajal, observed the ongoing conflict within the family. She admired her older sister but also felt the weight of their parents' expectations.

As the weeks went by, the drama within the family escalated. Arguments grew more heated, and Ananya's father, a stern and traditional man who placed a high value on their family's culture and traditions, remained unyielding in his stance against the love marriage. The emotional turmoil in the household was palpable, and it seemed that there was no easy solution in sight.

Ananya faced one of the most challenging periods of her life, caught between her love for Saameer and her family's deeply held beliefs. The drama and tension within her family showed no signs of abating, and Ananya knew that finding a resolution would not be easy.

As she returned to the city, the weight of her promise hung heavily on her heart. She knew that this was a dramatic turn of events in her love story, one that would test her love for Saameer and her commitment to her family's traditions.

Whispers of a Love Lost

Ananya's heart was a tempest of emotions as she returned to her family's home, burdened by the weight of their expectations and traditions. She knew that she had to meet Sameer, her beloved, one last time and share with him the heart-wrenching truth that threatened to tear her apart.

One evening, the sun began its descent, casting a warm, golden glow over the city, and Ananya and Sameer met at their cherished spot, a secluded park where their love had blossomed and thrived.

Ananya's eyes glistened with tears, like dewdrops clinging to the petals of a fragile flower. She took a deep, quivering breath and spoke, her voice a soft, trembling melody, *"Sameer, there's something I need to tell you."* Her words hung in the air like a delicate note, pregnant with the weight of their love. *"My family, they...they won't accept us. They want me to follow our traditions and culture, and they've asked me to promise that I'll never see you again."*

Sameer, his gaze locked onto Ananya's, felt his heart shatter into a million fragments. He reached out, his touch gentle as a whisper, and cradled her trembling hands. *"Ananya, I can't bear the thought of causing you pain. I know how deeply you love your family, and I can't bear to ask you to defy their wishes."*

Tears flowed freely down Ananya's cheeks, like a river of sorrow. She whispered, her voice breaking like a fragile dream, *"But... I can't bear the thought of losing you either, Sameer. You are my heart, my soul...., my very reason for being."*

Sameer, his thumb brushing away her tears, his voice a symphony of love and anguish, murmured, *"Ananya, I love you more than life itself. But I can't be the chain that binds your spirit. We both deserve to find our happiness."*

As the weight of their impossible situation pressed upon them, Ananya and Sameer clung to each other, their hearts entwined in a dance of love and despair. In that quiet park, beneath the fading sunlight that bathed their world in hues of gold and rose, they made a heart-rending decision, fueled by a love that defied fate.

Sameer, his voice quivering like the last leaf clinging to a tree in the throes of autumn, declared, *"Ananya, we must let each other go, set our hearts free."*

Ananya, her voice a fragile whisper carried by the evening breeze, nodded through her tears, unable to form words. They sealed their love with one last, fervent kiss, a bittersweet farewell to a love that destiny had conspired against. Then, slowly, reluctantly, they released each other's embrace, their souls forever marked by the indelible bond they shared.

As they parted, their tear-filled eyes locked for a final, lingering moment. *"Promise me, Ananya,"* Sameer implored, his voice quivering, *"that you'll carry the flame of our love in your heart."*

Ananya, her voice an ethereal echo, whispered through her tears, *"I'll never forget you, Sameer. You will always dwell in the deepest chambers of my soul."*

With hearts as heavy as the world itself, they turned away from each other, each step a painful journey in opposite directions. Their love, pure and profound, had been their refuge, but the world had forced them into an agonizing choice. Yet, as they walked away, they could not resist the pull of their hearts, and they rushed back into each other's arms, embracing fiercely, knowing that this moment would be their last.

Tears cascaded like a waterfall, and they held onto one another, hearts and souls entwined, as they embraced for the final time, a farewell marked by the most profound love and the most profound pain. Sameer's voice quivered as he said, *"Jao aaj ke baad mujhse kabhi mat milna, kahi baat mat karna,"* tears welled up in his eyes, his heart aching with the intensity of his emotions.

As they finally let go and walked away, their love story transformed into a poignant memory, a love that was never meant to be but would forever burn as an eternal flame in their souls.

Maatrishya Uvach

Mummy Kehti hai humari Chapter 13 verses 72, "*Life's dance is guided by love. It comforts our hearts and brings back our excitement when its music plays again.*"

In the intricate dance of life, love takes the lead. It guides our steps gracefully, soothes our souls with its tender melodies, and reignites our enthusiasm when its enchanting tune plays once more. In these cherished moments, we discover the profound beauty of our existence, finding joy in the embrace of our loved ones and comfort in the simple wonders that surround us.

Love's rhythm is like a timeless and enchanting song that accompanies us throughout life's many chapters. It offers solace, connection, and a deep sense of purpose. In the grand symphony of our lives, love is the sweet and enduring melody that makes every step of our journey worthwhile. It's the gentle hand that lifts us when we stumble, the warm embrace that celebrates our victories, and the unwavering presence that reminds us we are never truly alone.

As we gracefully waltz through the intricate ballroom of life, it's essential to remember that love isn't just an emotion; it's a powerful force that unites us. It transcends boundaries and forges connections that withstand the tests of time. With each step we take and every note of life's exquisite song, we should treasure the love that graces our path, finding solace in the knowledge that its melodious tune will persist, filling our hearts with its sweet resonance.

In the grand tapestry of existence, love's thread weaves through every moment, connecting us not only to our innermost selves but also to others. It's the laughter shared with dear friends, the tender moments with family, and the passion discovered in the arms of a beloved. Love serves as the anchor that grounds us and the wings that enable us to soar to greater heights.

However, it's important to acknowledge that love's dance isn't without its challenges. There will be moments when the music falters, and we may stumble along with it. But it's in these very moments that love's strength shines through. It's our resilience to rise after a stumble, our capacity to forgive and heal, and our unwavering determination to keep dancing, even when the steps seem uncertain.

So, in this grand ballroom of life, where love orchestrates both the music and the dance, let's twirl with grace. Let's embrace each and every note, knowing that love is our steadfast companion, our source of joy, and the most profound expression of our shared humanity. In each tender step, in every heartfelt gesture, and in the enduring bonds we nurture, we discover the true essence of our existence, where every moment becomes a testament to the beauty and power of the human heart.

So, dear friends, continue to dance on in the embrace of love's enduring melody. For it is in love's dance that we not only discover the true essence of our existence but also shape the world around us with its transformative power. With each step, with every heartfelt connection, we become the composers of a more loving and compassionate world.

Now, let's return to their story. Their journey stood as a testament to the profound beauty of existence, where they found joy in the embrace of their friendship and comfort in the simple wonders that surrounded them. Their connection, much like the sweet and enduring melody of a timeless song, gracefully guided their steps through the various chapters of their lives. Love provided solace, a deep sense of purpose, and unwavering support, even during moments of stumbling along the way.

In the intricate dance of life, where Sameer and Ananya's love took the lead, it guided their steps gracefully, soothing their souls with its tender melodies, and reigniting their enthusiasm when its enchanting tune played once more. In these cherished moments of their journey, they discovered the profound beauty of their existence, finding joy in the embrace of their friendship and comfort in the simple wonders that surrounded them.

Their love's rhythm resembled a timeless and enchanting song, accompanying them throughout life's many chapters. It offered solace, a deep connection, and a profound sense of purpose. In the grand symphony of their lives, love served as the sweet and enduring melody that made every step of their journey worthwhile. It was the gentle hand that lifted them when they stumbled, the warm embrace that celebrated their victories, and the unwavering presence that reminded them they were never truly alone.

As Sameer and Ananya gracefully waltzed through the intricate ballroom of life, they cherished the love that graced their path, finding solace in the knowledge that its melodious tune would persist, filling their hearts with its sweet resonance. Their journey was interwoven with moments of laughter, tender conversations, and the passion they discovered in their deepening friendship. Love served as the anchor that grounded them and the wings that enabled them to soar to greater heights.

Their story was not without its challenges and moments of uncertainty, but it was in those very moments that the strength of their bond truly shone. Their resilience, capacity to forgive and heal, and unwavering determination to keep dancing through life's ups and downs were a testament to the enduring power of their connection.

In the grand ballroom of their shared experiences, where love orchestrated both the music and the dance, Sameer and Ananya twirled with grace. They embraced each and every note, knowing that love was their steadfast companion, the source of their joy, and the most profound expression of their shared humanity.

In each tender step, in every heartfelt conversation, and in the enduring friendship they nurtured, Sameer and Ananya discovered the true essence of their existence. Their story became a testament to the beauty and power of the human heart, where their friendship and love for each other continued to shape their world with its transformative and enduring power.

What happens next, only two people know. One is me, and the other is time. I won't reveal it because my job is not to predict the future, and as for time, it is ready to tell, but it hasn't arrived yet. Some might wonder where I am, so let me clarify, I am Sarvvyapi.

Next Chapter

Ananya was sitting on the same bench where she used to meet Sameer, have conversations with him. One evening, a man arrived there and sat next to her. He smiled and said, *"Dil ki baat hai, aankhon se keh do, usse ab bhi mohabbat hai, ye sach keh do."* Divya asked, *"Aap kaun?"* He replied, *"Oh, mein... (laughs) Mein Aayush..."*

Epilogue

In the grand tapestry of life, where destiny often weaves intricate threads of suspense, there are moments when the unexpected becomes a harbinger of what lies ahead.

Years had passed since Ananya and Sameer had parted ways, their love silenced by the weight of tradition and duty. Each had moved forward with their lives, building new chapters, but the echoes of their past love still resonated deep within.

Ananya had become a renowned travel writer, her articles celebrated for their depth and insight into the world's most exotic destinations. She had found companionship in her life, someone who had understood her passion for adventure, but who also knew that a part of her heart still belonged to Sameer.

Sameer, on the other hand, had dedicated himself to his work in sustainable development, traveling the world to make a difference.

It was during one of Ananya's assignments that fate decided to intervene. She was in a remote village in South America, documenting the efforts of a local community to protect their pristine forests. Little did she know that this village was connected to Sameer's current project?

As she delved deeper into her work, Ananya started hearing whispers among the villagers about a foreigner who had come to their aid. They spoke of a man named Sameer, whose tireless efforts had made a significant impact on their lives.

Curiosity piqued, Ananya decided to inquire further. She described Sameer based on her memories, and the villagers confirmed that it was indeed the same man. Sameer had been silently working here, never mentioning his past, his lost love, or the sacrifice they had made.

Overwhelmed by a mix of emotions, Ananya knew she had to see him again, to thank him for the impact he was making in these people's lives. As she made her way to the village where Sameer was stationed, her heart raced with anticipation and uncertainty.
And then, in a small clearing surrounded by the lush green of the rainforest, they met again. Sameer, his eyes filled with surprise and disbelief, stood before Ananya. The years melted away, and for a moment, they were back in that quiet park, under the fading sunlight.

But there was something more, a sense of suspense in the air, as if destiny had more surprises in store for them. They didn't exchange words, for words felt inadequate to capture the depth of their emotions. Instead, they locked eyes, and in that shared gaze, they communicated everything that had remained unspoken for so long—love, regret, gratitude, and a profound sense of closure.

As they slowly turned away from each other, their eyes still locked, they carried with them the silent understanding that their paths had converged once again, not as lovers but as two souls forever connected by an unbreakable bond.

And so, as we conclude their story, we are reminded that in the grand tapestry of life, suspense often lingers around the corner, and destiny may have more surprises in store.

What lies ahead for Ananya and Sameer remains a tantalizing question, waiting to be unraveled.

Afterword

As we draw the curtains on the enthralling tale of Ananya and Sameer, we find ourselves reflecting on the powerful currents of love, tradition, and destiny that have coursed through their lives.

Their journey, filled with emotion and suspense, serves as a poignant reminder that love knows no bounds, yet often, it must navigate the complex terrain of familial expectations and societal norms.

While we've shared the dramatic chapters of their story, we must acknowledge that life continues to unfold beyond the pages of this narrative. Ananya and Sameer have moved forward, each on their own unique path, but the echoes of their love remain etched in their hearts.

The suspense of what lies beyond these pages, the twists and turns of their future, is a story only time can tell. Love, like destiny, has a way of surprising us when we least expect it.

And so, dear reader, we leave you with the knowledge that Ananya and Sameer's story continues to evolve, just as our own lives do. May their journey inspire you to embrace the suspense of your own narrative, for in it lays the beauty of life's unpredictability?

With warm regards,

Aayush Maatrishya

Acknowledgement

"Prem: Ek Sookha Phool"

I would like to express my heartfelt gratitude to everyone who contributed to the creation of the story *"Prem: Ek Sookha Phool."* This story would not have been possible without the support, inspiration, and dedication of many individuals.

First and foremost, I want to thank the *'Maate.'*

I extend my sincere appreciation to my family for their unwavering encouragement and belief in my writing. Your constant support has been my driving force.

To the readers of my work, your enthusiasm and passion for storytelling are my greatest motivation. Thank you for joining Sameer & Ananya Journey. Last but not least, I want to acknowledge the power of storytelling itself. It is a universal language that connects us all, and I am grateful to be a part of this beautiful tradition.

Very very thank you the *'Uncommon.'*

With heartfelt thanks,

Aayush Maatrishya

Aayush Maatrishya

Aayush Jha, known by his pen name Aayush Maatrishya, is an accomplished author who has earned a reputation for captivating readers with his thought-provoking narratives. With a keen eye for storytelling and a profound passion for literature, he has penned several engaging novels and short stories. His works traverse various genres, from gripping thrillers to heartwarming dramas, showcasing his versatility as a writer. Aayush's ability to craft compelling characters and weave intricate plots has not only won critical acclaim but also garnered him a dedicated following of avid readers.

Hailing from the vibrant city of Jamshedpur, Aayush draws inspiration from the lives and stories of the people in his community. He firmly believes in the transformative power of words and remains dedicated to inspiring and touching the hearts of readers through his literary creations.

Professional Career: Maatrishya professional journey has been intertwined with his passion for writing. He began his career as a poet, and over time, his interest turned to story writing.

Writing Style and Themes: Aayush Maatrishya is renowned for his evocative and immersive writing style. He weaves intricate narratives that delve into the complexities of human emotions and relationships. His works often explore themes of identity, true love, cultural diversity, and the human condition, resonating with readers on a profound level.

Conclusion: Aayush Maatrishya stands as a remarkable literary figure, known for his distinctive storytelling, exploration of universal themes, and his commitment to fostering cross-cultural empathy through his words. His works continue to inspire readers and contribute to the world of contemporary literature.

Books By This Author

Anjanne Ajnabee

"Anjanne Ajnabee" is a compelling tale of growth, reconciliation, and the human capacity to heal wounds. It serves as a poignant reminder that it's never too late to express gratitude, seek forgiveness, and free oneself from the burdens of unresolved emotions. Through Raahul's evolving narrative, readers are invited to join him on this transformative journey, encouraging introspection and offering a pathway toward inner peace and emotional freedom.